For Betsy Sachs, who tangos in the hay . . .
who rhumbas night and day . . .
—E. W.

For Luke and Lilly
—B. L.

Henry Holt and Company, LLC, *Publishers since 1866*
175 Fifth Avenue, New York, New York 10010
www.HenryHoltKids.com

Henry Holt® is a registered trademark of Henry Holt and Company, LLC.
Text copyright © 2001 by Elizabeth Winthrop
Illustrations copyright © 2001 by Betsy Lewin
All rights reserved.
Distributed in Canada by H. B. Fenn and Company Ltd.

Library of Congress Cataloging-in-Publication Data
Winthrop, Elizabeth.
Dumpy La Rue / by Elizabeth Winthrop; illustrated by Betsy Lewin.
Summary: A rhyming story about a pig whose passion for dancing becomes contagious.
[1. Dance—Fiction. 2. Pigs—Fiction. 3. Domestic animals—Fiction. 4. Stories in rhyme.]
I. Lewin, Betsy, ill. II. Title. PZ8.3.W727 Du 2000 [E]—dc21 99-53627

ISBN 978-0-8050-7535-9
7 9 10 8 6

First published in hardcover in 2001 by Henry Holt and Company
First paperback edition, 2004 / Designed by Martha Rago
The artist used black brush line and watercolor washes on Strathmore paper
to create the illustrations for this book.
Printed in July 2009 in China by South China Printing Company Ltd.,
Dongguan City, Guangdong Province, on acid-free paper. ∞

DUMPY LA RUE

Elizabeth Winthrop

ILLUSTRATED BY Betsy Lewin

HENRY HOLT AND COMPANY / NEW YORK

Dumpy La Rue wanted to dance.

"You're a pig," said his father.

"Pigs don't dance.

They grunt, they grovel,

they snuffle for truffles."

"Pigs don't dance,"
said his mother.
"They bellow, they swallow,
they learn how to wallow."

"I want to dance,"
said Dumpy.

"Fat chance," said his sister.
"Boys don't dance.
They fight, they march,
they sport, and they snort.
And they're never ever
supposed to cavort."

But Dumpy La Rue
was a pig
who knew what he wanted to do.

He twirled in the sty,
raised his snout to the sky,

spread his hooves far and wide,
and pretended to fly.

The cow came by.
Then the horse, and some fowl,
a mule, fourteen sheep, and a fox on a prowl.

A turkey all gobbling,
a goat and his mate,
and five gray rats, who were quite overweight.
They stopped and they stared.
They leaned on the fence.
'Twas the first time they'd seen
a pig who could dance.

"Hey, Dumpy, you're dancing,"
yelled the goose. "What a kick!"
She hopped up and down.
"You look pretty slick!"

Dumpy's father buried his snout.

Dumpy's mother tried to go out.

Dumpy's sister knocked off the flies,
sat down in the mud,
and covered her eyes.

But Dumpy La Rue
was clearly a pig
who knew what he wanted to do.

He slipped in the slop,
he slid in the slime.
But no matter what,
he always kept time.

He did a glissade,
a pas de bourrée.
From slop heap to bucket,
he jetéd his way.

"He's a porker with passion,
a dancing fool,
a pig with rhythm—
this breaks every rule,"
said the normally reticent mule.

"We want to dance too,"
cried the sheep.
"It looks fun.
Why should *he* be
the only one?"

"What's the tune?" yelled the cow.
"What's the beat?" called the horse.

"You can't hear it, of course,"
said Dumpy La Rue.
"It's all in my head.
You have it too.

If you want to dance,
if you want to glide,
just close your eyes
and listen inside."

The turkey stopped gobbling.
The barnyard grew quiet.
Even Poppa Pig decided to try it.

Some heard bugles,
some heard drums,
some heard mothers humming hums.

Some heard rhumbas,
some heard swing,
some heard choirs of angels sing.

Some heard jazz,
some heard blues,
some heard the slap of tapping shoes.

Then all of a sudden
in twos and in threes
the animals stirred
like leaves to a breeze.

The cow shimmied right.
The horse turned a twirl
till his long knobby legs
were curled in a curl.

The goats did a two-step.
The fox did a three.
The mule danced the salsa
with a neighboring tree.

The rats formed a line
and shuffled down the lane.
And when they reached the gate
they shuffled back again.

Poppa Pig waltzed Mama
all around the sty.
Even Dumpy's sister
bounced a little
on the sly.

"You were right," called his mother.
"You were right," cried his pop.
"Once you get us pigs a-dancing,
we don't ever want to stop."

Now his friends had learned to dance,
they would never be the same.

They would tango in the hay,
they would rhumba night and day.

Word would spread far and wide
of mules that twirl and sheep that glide.

Folks would come from high and low
to see this most amazing show.